T0198400

GABRIEL
AND THE
WISH KEEPER

BRENDA SILVERMAN

Archway Publishing books may be ordered through booksellers or by contacting:

Archway Publishing
1663 Liberty Drive
Bloomington, IN 47403
www.archwaypublishing.com
844-669-3957

ISBN: 978-1-6657-4536-9 (sc)
ISBN: 978-1-6657-4537-6 (e)

Print information available on the last page.

Archway Publishing rev. date: 06/22/2023

This book is dedicated to my unappreciated beautiful friend, Tracy and my son, William. It was while watching my son enjoying his own wish come true that this wonderful story came to me. Also, thank you Tracy's kindergarten class of 1999 in Belmont, CA for coming up with the name Wishem the planet wishes were born.

Thank you, Faye, for your wonderful support. You earned your wings on this project.

Contents

Gabriel is a young boy of eight and while other children are outside playing, he can only watch from his window. Sadly, Gabriel's heart is just not as strong as it needs to be. Today he isn't feeling like himself at all but he never shows it. He doesn't want to upset his parents. You see, Gabriel has always had a very weak heart, and now it seems his condition has worsened. His parents are preparing to take Gabriel to the doctor. Somehow, Gabriel knows this time he will not be coming home, so he puts on a brave face, smiles from ear to ear, and patiently waits.

"OK, Gabriel, time to go," his father says. He picks Gabriel up and places him in his wheelchair. His father notices the window is still open, so he reaches to shut it.

"Let me do it Dad," Gabriel says. He stands up and takes a long, deep breath, then he closes the window. As he sits back down, he looks around his room. Beautiful pictures of him with his parents are everywhere. He feels lucky to have such wonderful parents who love him so much.

His father wheels him to the front door. As they reach the ramp, Gabriel says, "Go fast, Daddy."

His father knows he likes to go down the wheelchair ramp fast. It tickles his tummy.

Gabriel is still giggling when his father places him in the car. He looks out of the window at his mother walking toward the car. She has a bag of goodies for their trip. She gets in the car, placing the snacks in the back seat. She says, "OK. Let's go. We do not want to be late."

It is well past six in the evening before the doctor can see Gabriel. All the tests have been done, and his parents eagerly await the results. Suddenly the doctor knocks on the door. "Well, hello, Gabriel."

"Hello, Dr. Evans." Gabriel yawns.

Doctor Evans says, "You must be exhausted from all the tests. Just relax now, Gabriel. I need to talk to your parents." He turns to Gabriel's mother and father. "Can you come to my office? I need to show you something." His parents are shocked at the doctor's request, but they agree. They look over at Gabriel. He is fast asleep. They follow the doctor to his office.

"Have a seat," the doctor says.

His parents sit down. "What is going on, doctor?"

"I am afraid the news is not good. Gabriel will not be leaving the hospital today. Has he been complaining about how he is feeling?" They both shake their heads. "Well, his condition is even worse than I imagined. He isn't going to make it much longer.

"What do you mean? He was OK this morning." His mother begins to cry.

Doctor Evans says, "Of course we will make him as comfortable as possible. We can set up a place next to Gabriel's bed so you can be with him."

"Should we tell him, doctor? Gabriel's father asks.

"That is entirely up to you. I have another patient, so I will say goodbye."

They both give Doctor Evans a hug and thank him for all he has done for Gabriel.

"I will be around if there is anything you need," Doctor Evans says.

Gabriel's parents take each other's hands and walk toward Gabriel's room. "Wait," his father says. "Let's take a walk outside first, to clear our heads."

His mother says, "What about Gabriel? He might wake up."

"He will be fine," his father says. As they walk outside, they notice the moon is full.

They see a bench close to the front door. Just as they sit down, they notice a shooting star falling from the sky. As it falls, they each make a wish. When they finish wishing, a bolt of lightning shoots through the sky, soaring well past the stars, like it has a purpose.

"What was that?" his father says.

"I don't know, but we better get back in before Gabriel wakes up," says his mother. They walk back into the hospital. When they reach Gabriel's room, he is still sleeping.

***

If you are wondering what that bolt of lightning was, one thing is for sure: that had never happened before. The wish made by Gabriel's parents was so full of love it shot right past the wish keepers and straight to the queen of Wishem herself.

Oh, wait. Let me back up. My name is Gilland. I am a wish keeper from a planet called Wishem. I am here to grant a wish. Now, can you keep a secret? OK then. This secret is thousands of years old. It's the secret of wishes. Have you ever wondered where a wish goes once you wished it? Or who hears that wish? What makes a wish come true? Well, I know the answers to those questions.

You see, there are wish keepers all over the earth. They're in place so when a wish is made, they can gather it up. They then take those wishes to Wishem, where the wise and beautiful Fairy Queen Lillianna decides if the wish deserves to come true. Our queen has been granting wishes for thousands of years for the people of Earth. Today something magical is going to happen. Not only will I grant these wishes, but I will be bringing the boy back with me.

***

The clouds part above Gilland's head. It's the queen. "Gilland, who are you talking to? Get a move on. The boy's time is drawing near," the queen says.

"Yes, my queen." Gilland turns around three times and transforms into an eagle. Stretching his wings wide, he ascends.

Gilland arrives at the hospital in the blink of an eye. He then perches on Gabriel's windowsill. Out of nowhere, a blue bird appears! It's the queen. She says, "Stop fooling around and get in there, Gilland!"

Gilland searches for a place to land. As he descends, he turns back into his true wish keeper self. He brushes the remaining feathers from his coat. As the last one falls, it disappears. He enters the hospital and heads toward Gabriel's room. When he reaches the room, he can see Gabriel's parents. They look sad.

Oh, one thing you should know: wish keepers are invisible. You can only see them if they want you to.

Gilland walks into the room. He stands next to Gabriel's mother and touches her shoulder.

Gabriel suddenly wakes up. "Hi Mom! Hi Dad!"

His parents smile. "Hello, Gabriel."

Gabriel sees a man dressed in all white standing next to his mother. "Mom, who is that man standing next to you?"

"What man?" his mother says.

"That man in the white suit standing next to you," says Gabriel.

His mother turns around. "There is nobody here, Gabriel. Where is he?"

"He is right there," exclaims the boy.

"No one is there, Gabriel. What does he want?" his mother asks.

"My mom wants to know what you want."

Gilland says, "I am here to grant their wishes."

Gabriel tells his parents, "He is granting wishes for you."

His parents look at each other. "What is his name?" his father says.

"I'm Gilland."

The boy says, "He said his name is Gilland. He wants me to go with him."

"Would you like to go with him?" his father asks.

"I guess so. Is it OK?"

"Sure, Gabriel. It's OK," says his father. "I am very tired right now though. Go back to sleep, Gabriel. We'll be right here when you get up."

"OK. I love you Mom and Dad."

"We love you too."

"Bye, Gilland," says Gabriel, and he quickly falls asleep again.

Beep, beep, beep go the monitors. Gabriel's heart has stopped. The doctor rushes in and listens to Gabriel's chest. There is no heartbeat. The doctor says with sadness, "I am so sorry. He is gone. Let me give you some time with him."

His parents know this day had to come, but they have been hoping to have more time. They both sit down next to Gabriel and cry. Then his mother asks, "What did you wish for?"

His father clears his throat. "I wished Gabriel could go to a wonderful place full of magic. There he would be happy and healthy. And you?"

"I wished he could go to a place where he could run and play. Somewhere full of as much love as we have for him. I will miss him so much. We both will," says his mother.

They sit with Gabriel hoping for a miracle, but there is no miracle on this day. Or would there be? They sit a little longer and then go home.

To Wishem

Suddenly Gabriel wakes up. He rubs his eyes. He cannot believe what he is seeing. It's the man in the white suit sitting on a bench just a few feet away. Gabriel sits down next to him.

"Hello, sir," Gabriel says.

"Well, hello there, Gabriel."

"Am I dreaming?" the boy asks.

"No, you are not dreaming," says Gilland.

"What is this place? Sir?"

"Call me Gilland."

"OK, Gilland. What is this place?"

"It is a waiting station."

"What are you waiting for?"

"A transport," says Gilland.

"A transport?" Gabriel is confused. "A transport to where?"

"Remember, we're going on a trip," says the wish keeper.

"Where are my parents?"

"They are back at the hospital."

"Do they know that I left?"

"Yes, Gabriel, they know. They wished this for you. You will be going on an adventure." "Wow! I will? Where to?"

"To Wishem. My queen is expecting your arrival."

"Will I be able to say goodbye to my parents?"

"You already have, Gabriel."

"How do you know my name?"

"It was on the wishes. Let me explain. I am a wish keeper."

"What's a wish keeper?"

"A wish keeper gather wishes. I am here to grant your parents' wishes."

Suddenly Gabriel hears a loud sound. "Do you hear that, Gilland? It sounds like something is coming this way. What is it?"

"You will see."

The sounds grow louder and louder and suddenly, smoke is everywhere. As the smoke clears, the doors of the transport open. A little man in a red coat steps out. He says, "Arriving Earth Station."

He must be the conductor, Gabriel thinks. When the doors are completely open, all manner of creatures start pouring out. There are fairies, sprite's, and a flying toad, trolls, witches, and a fairy godmother. Then a man walks out. He is spectacular. He has long blond hair and huge golden wings.

"Hello Markus."

"Oh hello Gilland."

"Busy night Markus?"

"Always. Who is this young man?"

"This is Gabriel. He is an Earth boy. The first to go to Wishem."

"Yeah, I heard about you. Have fun Gabriel."

"Thank you, Markus," says Gabriel.

Markus replies, "Well, I've got to go. Lots of people need me tonight. Bye Gilland. Nice to meet you Gabriel." He stretches out his beautiful wings and flies away.

"Where is he going?"

"Markus is a messenger fairy. He brings messages of hope to people who need it. What an excellent job he has. Yes, he is fortunate."

After everyone has departed, the conductor appears again. He rings his bell, then shouts, "All aboard, all aboard the express transport to Wishem. All fairy toads and tinker tabs please leave the transport; this is an express. Tinker tabs and fairy toads please board on track two." When he says that, all the tinker tabs and fairy toads rush off as fast as they can.

"Why can't they ride?" Gabriel asks.

"They cannot travel the wormhole highway."

"Why not?"

"Gabriel, you do not want to see what happens to them once they're inside the wormhole."

"Oh," he says.

Again, the conductor shouts, "All aboard. All leprechauns to the rear please. Everyone else have your seats; we will be leaving momentarily." It is strange, but fairies and other creatures are coming out of nowhere and boarding the transport. Gabriel even sees Prince Charming.

"OK Gabriel, let's find a seat."

They find one right behind a leprechaun and his son. Gabriel can't help but stare at the leprechaun. When the leprechaun notices, he tells Gabriel it is not polite to stare.

"Oh, I am sorry. It's just I've never seen a leprechaun before. I'm Gabriel."

The leprechaun gives Gabriel a dirty look. "I'm Peter."

"Hi Peter." Peter's father then tells him to turn around.

"How does the transport move Gilland?"

"This transport runs on the power of wishes."

"Wow," Gabriel says.

"Buckle up. We are about to leave."

Gabriel fastens his seat belt.

"Here we go." The transport begins to move, but it is not going forward. It is going up. It rises slowly at first then shoots like a bullet toward the moon.

"Hold on Gabriel."

Gabriel holds on tightly.

"Look out at the window, Gabriel."

He cannot believe what he sees. "We're in space. I can see the moon."

Gilland smiles. Suddenly, the conductor makes an announcement that they are about to approach the wormhole highway.

"Hold on, Gabriel."

Now they are going so fast that Gabriel begins to get dizzy. Gilland can tell Gabriel is not feeling particularly well. He reaches into his pocket, pulls out a purple piece of what looks like candy, and gives it to Gabriel. "Here, take this. You will feel better."

"Thank you, Gilland." He eats it and feels better at once. The transport begins to slow down. "Are we there, Gilland?"

"Not yet Gabriel."

The conductor announces, "We will be in Wishem in five minutes, so please have your food ready for the Widget as you depart."

Gabriel looks worried. "Food for the Widget? What is a Widget, Gilland?"

"The Widget is our gate keeper. You cannot get into Wishem without first feeding him."

"What does he eat?"

"The food he needs is the food of knowledge. You must tell him something he has never heard before."

"What shall I say?"

"Do not worry. You will think of something."

As they leave the transport, the first one off is Prince Charming. It seems he's forgotten he has to feed the Widget. As he steps forward, the Widget asks him, "What have you got for me, Prince?"

"Will a fine gold coin do?"

With a loud booming voice, the Widget says, "What? You have forgotten. Guards!"

Suddenly, two trolls in guards' uniforms step up. One takes the horse, the other Prince Charming.

"Back to the enchanted forest with you. You're lucky I do not banish you—forever."

Gilland and Gabriel step up.

"Hello Gilland." The Widget is happy to see him. "What tasty morsel do you have for me today?"

Gilland whispers in his ear and the Widget laughs so hard he cries. "You may pass." The Widget nods to the guard at the gate and Gilland walks through.

A little frightened, Gabriel steps up.

"What are you supposed to be?" the Widget asks.

"I'm Gabriel. I'm from Earth."

"All right Gabriel from Earth. What do you have for me?"

The only thing Gabriel can think of is a song his mom used to sing—so, he sings "Twinkle, Twinkle, Little Star." The Widget loves it so much he asks Gabriel to sing it again. After he finishes, the Widget lets Gabriel through the gate.

"I knew you could do it, Gabriel." Gilland puts his arm around Gabriel. "Tell me, how do you feel?"

"Well, I'm not sure. I've never felt this way before."

"What way, Gabriel?"

"Well, I feel kind of great. What's going on?"

"This is what you call a wish come true. The moment you entered Wishem you became one of us. The magic of our planet healed you."

"Oh, Gilland, thank you."

"Do not thank me. Thank your parents. It is their wishes that brought you here. Gabriel, you must promise me something: never tell anyone where Wishem is."

"Why, Gilland?"

"We do not want any bad wishes to get into Wishem. It would be devastating."

"OK," he says. "You can trust me. Who would want to hurt Wishem?"

"I can think of someone. He is a jealous wish master, a genie with great power. He thinks his way of granting wishes should be the only way. He has gotten in before. It was a mess."

"You have my word, Gilland." They finally reach the entrance.

Gilland opens the huge doors. "Welcome to Wishem."

As the door opens, Gabriel is amazed at the wondrous beauty of Wishem. He takes a minute and looks around. There are fairies with brightly colored wings tending to the most beautiful flowers he has ever seen. Chubby little tinker tabs collect garbage for dinner. There are unicorns and wild horses with multicolored wings. He recognizes the fairy toads. He watches as they fly from lily pad to lily pad. Suddenly, Gabriel feels the love of Wishem growing inside him.

"OK, Gabriel, we have an appointment to keep. We must hail a coach to the palace." Gabriel notices there are signs everywhere, all in rainbow colors, announcing a festival—a wishing flower festival.

"Gilland, what is a wishing flower?"

"Oh, it's our most treasured flower. It's blooming in a couple of days. When it blooms, the seeds float up in the air. If you catch one, you can make a wish. One thing though: you must make a wish for someone else."

"That's neat, Gilland."

"Yes, because it's the unselfish wish that is likely to come true."

"Those signs sure are colorful. Aren't they?"

"The leprechauns oversaw decoration this year. They do love a rainbow." Gilland whistles and a beautiful carriage with two flying unicorns appears.

"Where to, sir?"

"To the palace please." They both get in.

The coachman touches the reins and the unicorns' wings lift to catch the wind. Now Gabriel can really see the beauty of Wishem. Overwhelmed, Gabriel watches out the window then says, "Gilland, Wishem is awesome."

The coach descends right in front of the palace.

Gabriel Meets the Queen

As they step out of the carriage. Gabriel can't believe where he is.

"Gilland, are you sure I'm not dreaming?"

There are guards at the castle door. Gilland tells them the queen is expecting him.

"OK, follow me."

As they walk to the queen's throne room, Gabriel sees himself in a mirror hanging on the wall. Gilland looks. Gabriel is amazed at how healthy he looks.

The guard announces Gilland's arrival.

The queen stands. "Hello Gilland."

He bows, then says, "Hello, my queen."

"This must be Gabriel."

Still bowing, he says, "Yes, my queen."

"Come closer boy. Let's get a good look at you. How are you feeling?"

"I'm feeling very good, thank you."

"It seems Wishem magic has had a positive effect on you. Do you know why you are here Gabriel?"

"Well, something about wishes my parents made, I think."

"That's right. Your parents' love for you is so very strong, when they both wished for you at the same time, those wishes came directly to me. That has never happened before. So, I thought I must meet this human because he must be very special, and it seems you are, Gabriel."

"Thank you, Queen Lillianna."

The queen notices that Gabriel has a tear in his eye. "What is wrong Gabriel?"

"It's just that I miss my parents. Will I ever see them again?"

"Of course, you will."

"How?"

"Fairy magic, of course. Let's not get ahead of ourselves.

"Gabriel, I have a very important question to ask you. Because of your kind and gentle heart and the wishes that have been made for you, I, as queen of Wishem, invite you to live with us and become the first wish keeper from earth."

Gabriel looks at Gilland and smiles.

"You don't have to give me an answer now. Think about it. We will talk again soon. Gilland."

"Yes, my queen."

"Take him to Tailor Street. He will need some new attire. Then show him to his quarters."

"Yes, my queen."

"That is all. Oh, one thing: welcome to Wishem, Gabriel."

Butterman's Tailor Shop

They both bow and set off to get Gabriel some new clothes. When they are outside the palace, Gilland whistles for the coach; it seems it had been waiting for them.

As the coachman opens the door, he says, "Where to, sir?"

"Take us to Tailor Street."

"Right away, sir." The unicorns rise, fan their wings, and off they go. When they reach Tailor Street, the coach descends.

"Will that be all, sirs?"

"Yes, thank you."

They step out and walk toward a shop. The name on the shop is Butterman's. Gilland opens the door. Gabriel can see a butterfly as tall as a man behind the counter.

"Hello Gilland."

"Hello Mr. Butterman. We need an entire wardrobe suited for a wish keeper in training."

Butterman comes from behind the counter. He looks Gabriel up and down.

"What manner of creature are you?"

"This is Gabriel. He is from Earth."

"What are you supposed to be?"

"I guess I'm a human, sir."

"A human." Butterman rolls his eyes and shakes his head. "Now I have seen it all."

"All right, Butterman, settle down. Can you help us?"

"I guess we can make him something proper. Come with me boy."

Gabriel looks at Gilland, a little afraid.

You'll be OK, Gabriel. He won't hurt you."

"Well, come on human."

They disappear to the back of the store so Gabriel can be fitted.

While Gabriel is being fitted, Gilland sees an old friend. He steps outside and crosses the street. He sits down underneath a giant oak tree.

"Hello, wise oak," he says.

The tree opens his eyes. "Hello there, old friend. It's been quite a while, Gilland."

"Yes, it has."

"You look troubled, Gilland."

"I am a little."

"Maybe I can help, my friend. It's about the Earth boy, isn't it?"

"Yes."

"You're afraid the Wishem folk won't accept him."

"How did you know?"

"It's written all over your face. Gilland, let me ask you a question. Does a leprechaun worry about where the next rainbow will be?"

"No, I guess not."

"You're right. I have it on good authority that the Earth boy is going to do wonderful things. In time, he will capture the heart of all Wishem."

Gilland sighs with relief. "Thank you, wise old friend."

"Anytime, Gilland. You better get back in there. Butterman already has issues."

"Yes, you're right." Gilland walks back only to see Gabriel has already finished being measured and is thanking Butterman for his help.

"Where do I send his wardrobe?"

"To Fairy Towne. Give them to Hailey the house pixie. Tell her to put them in Gabriel's room."

"OK, Gilland. Now get out of here. I have work to do."

A coach pulls up.

"Never mind, coachman, we will be flying."

"What!" Gabriel says.

"Wouldn't you like to fly there?"

"Why yes, but I don't know how, Gilland."

"You'll be OK. Just hold on to me."

"All right."

Gilland pulls something out of his coat pocket. It's a small pouch. He opens it and sprinkles some kind of dust on Gabriel.

"What's that, Gilland?"

"It's pixie dust. It's magical. You'll be able to fly now. It's very powerful, so you just need a little."

"OK." Gabriel holds on to his hand and the next thing you know, they're flying.

"We will be there after we get something for Gabriel to eat. Thanks again, Butterman."

"You're welcome, Gabriel."

House of Delights

"**G**abriel, try not to look down."

"Why?" He accidentally looks down and begins to fall. Gilland catches him.

"That's why."

"Oh man, that was scary."

They descend slowly to the ground right in front of House of Delights.

"I'd like to do that again, Gilland."

"OK, but let's eat first."

They walk in. At once, Gabriel notices the host is young dragon. He looks at Gilland. "He won't hurt us, will he?"

"No, of course not. He's a water dragon."

"A water dragon? I've never heard of a water dragon. What do they do?"

"Well, when they are not putting out fires, they like to help out here. The food is good, and you never know when a fire might break out in the kitchen. Now let's have a seat."

As they wait for their server, Gabriel looks around the room. Everything is so beautifully decorated.

"What do you think about becoming a wish keeper, Gabriel?"

"I think I'd like it very much."

"Great. I will let the queen know in the morning. She will be so pleased. Have you thought about what you want for lunch? Yes, good here comes our server. Hello Amahia."

"Hey there, Gilland. Who's your friend?"

"His name is Gabriel."

"Hello. First time here?"

"Yes," he says.

"Let me tell you how it works. First, you think about what you want, then the cook will make it just the way you like it."

Gabriel closes his eyes.

Amahia asks, "Will that be a large or small chocolate milk?"

"Large, please."

"And you, Gilland?"

"The usual: peanut butter and apples with a small tea."

"Coming right up."

Amahia goes to the kitchen and returns with a huge plate of spaghetti with giant meatballs and a large glass of chocolate milk. She puts them in front of Gabriel. She also sets down Gilland's apples, peanut butter, and hot tea.

"Wow! Those meatballs are the size of baseballs!"

Gilland smiles. "Dig in, Gabriel."

Hungry, Gabriel gobbles it up in no time flat. When he looks up, he has spaghetti sauce all over his face.

Gilland laughs, then pulls a small mirror from his pocket. He shows Gabriel and they both laugh uncontrollably.

Amahia returns to the table. "Was everything satisfactory?"

"It was. Thank you, Amahia."

"Anytime."

Gabriel's New Home

"All right, let's get you to your new home."

"Can we fly to it, Gilland?"

"Sure, Gabriel."

As they fly high above Wishem, Gabriel is happy that his parents wished such a wonderful wish for him. Wishem is a wonderful place to be.

"Gilland, when is the Wishing Flower Festival?"

"It's in a couple of days. Worry not, Gabriel, I'll see to it you get there. But now you must get some sleep. You have your first class tomorrow. Hold on." They descend right in front of Gabriel's new home. And who is there to greet them? Haiely the house pixie. She is excited to see the boy everyone is talking about. She flies right up to Gabriel and introduces herself.

"Hello, Gilland," she says. "Is this Gabriel?"

"Yes, Gabriel meet Hailey. She'll be your house pixie."

"Oh. Hello, Hailey. Nice to meet you."

"Wow, he has good manners. Follow me Gabriel. I'll show you to your room."

"OK."

"Gabriel, I'll see you in the morning. All right Gilland." Hailey escorts Gabriel to his room. "We will be taking elevator." They step in, and Hailey pushes the button for the thirty-seventh floor. "So how do you like our planet, Gabriel?"

"Oh, it's beautiful. I really like it here."

Hailey smiles. When the elevator door opens, Hailey directs Gabriel down a long hall.

"Here we are." She opens his door. "Come in," she says. "I put you clothes away for you." She shows him the closet.

"Thank you, Haliey."

"Oh, the queen sent this package over for you. I put it on your bed."

"Thank you again, Hailey."

"You are so polite. You'll make a good wish keeper."

"Thank you Hailey."

"See you around, Gabriel." She flies out, leaving a trail of pixie dust behind her.

Box of Minnah

Gabriel loves his room. He finds his nightclothes and changes. He notices the box the queen has sent to him. He gets into bed and begins to open it. Inside the box is another box. He takes the box out and on the top of the box, it says "The Magical Box of Minnah." Gabriel notices the queen has written a note, so he opens it.

"This box is one of a kind. It has had many owners, but none of them could follow its simple instructions. The box has remained hidden for many years awaiting a worthy heart. Then and only then will you be given the instructions you need to use it."

Suddenly, a note is pushed under Gabriel's door. He gets out of bed and picks it up. The note reads, "You have been enrolled in flying lessons with Queen Rhoen at the Lily Pad Grounds. Class begins at ten o clock sharp."

Gabriel is very excited to start classes so soon. He knows he should go right to bed, so he places the box on the floor and turns off his light. Gabriel tosses and turns but cannot get the box of Minnah off his mind. He is so curious about its magic that he cannot resist. He reaches for the box and places it on his lap. He notices there is something written on the side. It says, "Hold the box in your hands and close your eyes. If the box opens, reach inside and get the instructions."

Curiosity gets the best of him. He picks up the box and closes his eyes. The box begins to shake and lights shoot out of the bottom. Scared, he puts it down. The box continues to shake for a minute then pops open. Gabriel slowly looks inside. There is a piece of paper that reads "Instructions." He slowly reaches in and grabs it. When he does, the box shuts right away.

The instructions are very simple.

1. Tell the box what it is you wish to look at.

2. Where it is, the box can find it.

3. Open the box, holding it in both hands, and look inside as the box reads your thoughts. It will show you what you wish to see.

At the bottom of the instructions is a warning that reads, "Never ever try to contact the person or persons you have reached, or the box will cease to work and disappear forever.

P.S. The Box of Minnah should be kept in a secret place of your choosing. Treasure it."

Gabriel yawns. He knows he has to get up early, but he really misses his parents. *Just one peek and I'll go to sleep*, he thinks.

He follows the instructions on the box. As the smoke clears, he can see his parents. It is dinnertime, and they are having Gabriel's favorite: big meatballs and spaghetti. They have set a place for Gabriel with his favorite teddy bear in his seat. He notices his mom is getting bigger—well, her tummy is. Before she sits down to eat, his dad pulls her chair out.

That's weird, he thinks. *I hope she's not sick.* Gabriel must go to bed so he closes the box, puts it high on his shelf behind some books, and goes to sleep,

It is not long before morning arrives. Suddenly there is a knock on his door. It is Gilland.

"Rise and shine, Gabriel. You don't want to be late for your first day of school."

Gabriel dresses hurriedly.

"Let's get some breakfast first." Gilland sprinkles pixie dust on Gabriel and off they go. When they arrive, the young dragon is not there. In his place is Anasha, a water fairy.

"Where is the dragon, Gilland?" Gabriel asks.

"Oh, they sleep during the day, Gabriel."

They are seated and awaiting their breakfast when Gilland notices that Gabriel looks tired.

"Something on your mind Gabriel?"

"Well yes, I was looking in the box"

"The Box of Minnah?"

"Yes, and I saw my parents. They seemed happy enough, but my mother seemed different. Her tummy has grown very large, and my father was acting funny."

"Oh, I see," Gilland says. "Well Gabriel, it appears your mother is going to have a baby soon."

Gabriel is surprised when he hears this. "Are you sure?"

"Yes, Gabriel, very sure. It's a girl. Your sister will be here soon. You're going to be a big brother."

Their food arrives and they eat quickly.

"Well, let's get a move on, Gabriel. You've got class in twenty minutes."

"All right, Gilland." As they fly, Gabriel looks worried.

"What's on your mind, Gabriel?"

"Do you think they will forget about me?"

"No, they will never forget you. They will always love you."

"Are you sure?"

"Yes, now stop worrying. You have class, and we are here."

Gabriel sees the other students rushing to get to class and follows them.

"Bye Gilland."

"I'll let the queen know you are taking your classes. She'll be very pleased."

"Thank you Gilland." Gabriel goes inside.

Gabriel Learns to Fly

He finds a seat in the back.

"Hi Gabriel."

He turns around and sees the leprechaun he met on the transport. "Oh, hi Peter. What are you doing here?"

"Leprechauns must fly as well. Of course, I'll be riding rainbows. Where is the teacher?"

Before Gabriel can blink an eye, in flies the biggest ladybug he has ever seen. She flies over them, knocking pencils and paper onto the floor with her giant wings.

"Our teacher's a Ladybug?" Gabriel says.

"What's that young man? And what in Wishem are you supposed to be?"

"Oh, I'm Gabriel."

"Yes, go on."

"From Earth."

"Are you a fairy?"

"Well, no I'm human."

"Oh, human. That explains a lot. Try to be quiet will you, human."

Gabriel sits up and is quiet as a mouse.

"OK class, eyes forward. My name is Queen Rohen. I am queen of the ladybugs here on Wishem and your teacher. Before you leave my class, you will be flying—well, most of you will. There may be some of you who just won't get it. Those who can't, try again next year. OK, let's begin. Everyone stand up. We are going outside." Rhoen flies out first with the class right behind her. "OK, the magic of flying comes from a place deep, deep inside. Now, I want all of you to close your eyes."

They all close their eyes.

"I want you to imagine that you are on a cloud. Keep your eyes closed. How many can see yourself floating?"

Most of the class raise their hands.

"Now believe—believe with all of your heart you can fly. This is the key, class: you must believe you can fly, and you will."

Suddenly Gabriel is floating above the class, then most of the class is floating.

"Those who are having trouble, stay focused and believe."

Now all of the class, except one boy, is floating.

"Good job everyone. Now touch back down. Let's take a break. Back inside in ten minutes."

"Hey Peter, did you see me?"

"Yeah, you're going to be flying in no time. It seemed easy for you, Peter."

"I guess," he says.

"But it's nothing like riding a rainbow to its end."

"I bet," Gabriel says.

"You are going to be a great wish keeper, Gabriel."

"Thank you, Peter. We better get inside."

As they step inside, they see Gunther talking to the teacher.

"That's the boy who didn't make it off the ground, Gabriel."

"Oh yeah." He looks sad as he leaves the classroom.

"All right class, I told you not everyone can be a wish keeper. Not every leprechaun can ride a rainbow. He is gone, and you are here. Now let's put what you have learned to the test."

Peter pays careful attention.

"Flying has three important components. It's one part imagination, one part expectation, and, most important part of all, you must believe. The power of believing is stronger than you know. Without it, you cannot ride a rainbow or fly above the clouds. Do you understand, class?"

"Yes," the class replies.

"Peter, take the other leprechauns and shows them how to ride a rainbow. Don't forget your maps. Everyone else, open your desks there you will find your assigned stations. Each wish keeper is assigned territory where he or she will gather wishes. Until that day, fly. Practice makes perfect. When you feel you've got it down, come back inside for your certification. Your next class is in two hours with Professor Hoppenstein."

The class goes outside for two hours. They fly all over Wishem.

While Gabriel is flying, he sees a cloud—a rain cloud. *It looks like a storm is coming*, he thinks. *Maybe I should let somebody know.* He touches down by Butterman's shop and who is there? Gilland.

"Hey Gilland."

"Hi Gabriel. I see you're flying."

Gabriel, out of breath, says, "A storm is coming."

"No, you're mistaken Gabriel. There hasn't been a storm on Wishem in at least seven hundred years."

"I've got to get to class, but see for yourself." Gabriel flies off to class.

Gilland looks up, and Gabriel is right. There are rain clouds forming. He rushes to tell the queen, "This storm could ruin the festival, or worse. It could be Thereon the genie."

Gabriel returns to class, He walks up to the ladybug Queen Rhoen and thanks her for the lessons.

"You're very welcome," she says. "Good luck, Gabriel. Be careful up there."

"I will," he says.

"Don't forget your letter of certification." She hands Gabriel his certification letter.

Gabriel then sits down and waits for the next class to start.

Professor Hoppenstein
Transformation

Professor Hoppenstein arrives. Surprisingly, he is a giant grasshopper with glasses on his nose and a top hat. When he speaks, he has a funny accent. "OK class, my name is Professor Hoppenstein. I'll be teaching you to transform. It's very simple to transform. You must first learn to listen. Can someone tell me what is the most important thing a wish keeper must do?"

The fairy in the back raises her hand. "Fly?"

"Very good dear, but no. Anyone else? No? All right then. A wish keeper must listen for he or she holds the key to their hopes and dream. To listen, you must first be still, not only in your body but in your mind as well. As you ponder this, I will show you. Take a deep breath, then another, and another. Close your eyes and listen to the sounds you hear. Block them out, until the only sound you hear is the beating of your heart."

The professor becomes so still you can hear a pin drop. Then poof—he becomes a feather.

"Now everyone, together take a deep breath, keeping your eyes closed. Take another. Feel the calm growing inside you. Breathe deeper. Calm your mind think of nothing at all. Take another breath. Transform."

Gabriel transforms into a blue bird. The fairy is a Widget. Everyone is transforming. It is crazy.

"As you transform, you must always remember to keep listening to your heart. It seems you've got it Now remember, the more you practice, the better you get. When you are finished, come get your certification. The festival starts in one hour."

One by one, the students receive their certifications then leave for the festival. Gabriel cannot believe how easy it is to transform. As he waits for Gilland, he continues to practice.

Gilland is still busy with the queen, discussing what action to take.

"Gilland, I think it's Theron the genie. We must make sure, of course, so this is what I want you to do. Go and get Alyssa, my sister. She is the only fairy who can find out if Theron's up to his old tricks. She'll be with the water fairies watering the queen's garden. Go quickly and bring her to me. On you way, tell Gabriel I wish to see him. I have a job for him. Now quickly go. There's no time to lose."

Gilland flies as fast as he can to the Lily Pad Grounds and lets Gabriel know the queen's request. He leaves at once for the castle while Gilland is off to find Alyssa.

The storm is now raging. The wind is starting to destroy all of the decorations for the festival. The Wishem folks are worried. Some have never seen a storm before.

Gabriel arrives at the castle. The queen asks him to go back to the festival and inform the head gardener of the storm. "He will tell the emergency storm team to be on high alert. I will meet you there when I've spoken to my sister."

"Right away, my queen."

As Gabriel leaves to inform the gardener, Gilland finds Alyssa and descends.

"Alyssa, I'm glad I found you. As you can see, there is a storm. The queen thinks it's Theron."

"That devil," she says.

"She has requested your help."

"I'm on my way."

Alyssa speeds toward the castle. She rushes past the guards. "My queen, have I heard correctly? Is Theron back?"

"Oh, sister, I believe he is. Will you help us?"

"Of course. I'll let you know when I find him."

"Thank you sister."

Alyssa flies high above Wishem. She needs to get a good look. She sees something out of place, and she descends to get a better look. It is a purple and gold bush, and it is smoking, creating the storm clouds above him. She quietly sneaks up on him and, with her fairy magic, ensnares him. As soon as she does, Thereon becomes angry and tries to free himself, but Alyssa's magic is too strong. Alyssa knows this magic won't last long over a genie, so she hurries back to the queen.

In the meantime, the storm damages the festival grounds and one of the wishing flower seeds flies off Wishem. The queen is alerted, but it is too late. It finds a wormhole and is now on its way to earth.

Gilland finds Gabriel at the festival. Gilland looks at the damage.

"Oh my, Gilland, look at the damage the storm has caused."

"I'll call for all tinker tabs to begin cleaning the grounds." Gilland pulls out a funny looking flute, plays a few notes, and all at once tinker tabs are everywhere, cleaning the grounds.

"Wow, look at them go. They're amazing. Gilland, is the festival over?"

"I'm afraid so, Gabriel. Remember I told you about Theron the genie?"

"Yes."

"Well, it was his magic that did this. The queen's sister Alysea found him. He is at the castle right now."

Alyssa arrives at the castle with Theron. The queen knows fairy magic will not hold a genie for long, so she is prepared. She takes a sacred jar from her shelf. As Theron is brought into the throne room, Alyssa holds him while the queen traps the evil genie in the jar and closes the lid tightly.

"I've got you, Theron," she says.

"Not for long," he grumbles. "Ha Haha, I've ruined your festival. No wishes today, Queen."

Alyssa gets the guards to watch Theron while go to the festival grounds. All of Wishem must be wondering what's going on. The guards stand watch as Alyssa and the queen take a coach to the festival. Once there, Gilland and Gabriel are brought to the queen.

"I must make an announcement." The queen stretches out her big, beautiful wings and flies above the people of Wishem. All eyes are on her.

"Kind Wishem folks, please calm yourselves. The storm is over. The blame for this disaster belongs to Theron the Genie. We have him trapped at the castle. He will be punished. I would like you to all know that Gabriel was the one who alerted us about the storm. Gabriel, come forward."

Everyone is cheering. The queen pulls a wand from her gown and touches Gabriel's head.

"Kneel, Gabriel. I, as queen of Wishem, do decree that, from this day forward, you are a wish keeper, the first of your kind. May this day go down in the history of Wishem for all time. Stand, Gabriel; you are one of us."

All of Wishem cheers.

"I must go now and deal with Theron. Gabriel and Gilland, meet me at the castle."

The queen flies back to the castle and the Wishem folks continue to celebrate.

"I guess Theron didn't ruin everything."

"You're right, Gabriel. He did not."

Gabriel is so happy to be a wish keeper.

"Gilland, I'm a wish keeper."

"Yes, Gabriel. I am so very happy for you. I wonder what the queen wants?"

"As do I."

At the palace, the queen commands that Theron be buried one hundred feet down in the queen's garden. The guards begin to dig.

"Theron won't bother Wishem for quite a while."

Gilland and Gabriel are announced. The queen is happy to see them.

"Gabriel, how would you like to have earth to watch over? They can always use a good wish keeper."

"Really! Well, I would like that a lot."

"That's good, because I have a mission for you."

Confused, Gilland asks, "My queen, is he ready?"

"Well, he will need some counseling. I have a task for both of you. It seems Theron's storm has done a lot more damage than you know. A seed has been detected on earth. It was blown into a wormhole during the storm and I need you to retrieve it. Will you do this for me?"

"Of course we will."

"Then prepare. You must leave at once."

As Gabriel prepares for his trip, he would like to tell you that you too can be a wish keeper. It is in the service of others that you feel the love of a wish come true. Next time you make a wish, make it for someone less fortunate. As Gilland said, it's the unselfish wish that is likely to come true. We will see you soon. Look for our next adventure, *Gabriel and the Wishing Flower*.

Printed in the United States
by Baker & Taylor Publisher Services